PARKER LOOKS UP

For my little sister, Ava

—P. C.

For my Aunt Sandy (Curry), who inspired us to share
Parker's story as a picture book

—J. C.

To Parker Curry—you are a prime example of how one person's experience
can touch the hearts of so many. Through your experience, I have been
blessed with the opportunity to continue to do what I love most—living my
childhood dream of being an illustrator. For that, I am eternally grateful.
Thank you for the opportunity to draw you, your family, and your friends,
and for allowing me to be a part of this wonderful ongoing journey.

—B. J.

ALADDIN
An imprint of Simon & Schuster Children's Publishing Division
1230 Avenue of the Americas, New York, New York 10020
First Aladdin hardcover edition October 2019
Text copyright © 2019 by Jessica Curry and Parker Curry
Illustrations copyright © 2019 by Brittany Jackson
For information about special discounts for bulk purchases, please contact Simon & Schuster Special Sales
at 1-866-506-1949 or business@simonandschuster.com.
The Simon & Schuster Speakers Bureau can bring authors to your live event. For more information or to book an event
contact the Simon & Schuster Speakers Bureau at 1-866-248-3049 or visit our website at www.simonspeakers.com.
Book designed by Laura Lyn DiSiena
The illustrations for this book were rendered digitally.
The text of this book was set in Filson Soft.
Manufactured in the United States of America 0919 PHE
10 9 8 7 6 5 4 3 2 1
Library of Congress Control Number 2019938117
ISBN 978-1-5344-5186-5 (hc)
ISBN 978-1-5344-5187-2 (eBook)

PARKER LOOKS UP

An Extraordinary Moment

By **Parker Curry** & **Jessica Curry**

Illustrated by **Brittany Jackson**

ALADDIN

New York   London   Toronto   Sydney   New Delhi

PARKER CURRY loved to dance.

Dressed in her favorite tutu, she imagined she was a dancing queen.

But one rainy Tuesday, instead of going to dance class, Parker's mom said,

Let's go to the museum.

Ava, too!

Parker loved visiting the museum almost as much as she loved twirling and leaping in the air.

She pulled on her boots,

Mom and her sister, Ava, buttoned up their jackets,

Have fun, girls!

Bye, Dad!

and off they went,

splashing and smiling and . . .

Gia, Parker's best friend, greeted them from the top of the museum steps.

Once inside, the friends hurried down a long
hall, looking at the paintings all around them.

They saw
**PRANCING
HORSES,**

BLOOMING FLOWERS,

A BUSHY
MUSTACHE,

A SHINY JEWELED NECKLACE,

TWO
PEACOCKS
WITH RED
EYES,

and **A BASKET OF SLIMY FISH**.

And **FEATHERS.**

Lots and lots of
BRILLIANT FEATHERS.

When Gia spotted a playroom, she raced ahead.
Parker charged after her.

Explore!

Let's make silly faces!

After Gia stuck purple hair onto the easel and Parker added a pirate hat and sunglasses, it was time to go home.

Time to go, girls!

Skipping down the hall, the girls spied a row of

FRILLY WHITE TUTUS.

Parker raised her arms.

Gia spun around and around and around.

"Wait for me!" Parker called, dancing after her friend until . . .

She froze in her tracks, spellbound.

PARKER CURRY LOOKED UP.

A portrait of First Lady Michelle Obama loomed before her.

She had rich brown skin, just like Parker, and kind, familiar eyes that reminded Parker of . . .

her mother,

her grandmother,

her sister,

and yes—even of herself.

How could someone look so real and so magical all at the same time?

Who is SHE?

MOTHER, LAWYER, WRITER, CARING, HERO, FRIEND, SISTER,

Parker's mother's voice filled the air, her words coming to rest squarely on Parker's tiny shoulders.

COURAGEOUS, SMART, INSPIRATIONAL, CONFIDENT, DYNAMIC, ADVOCATE, HONEST, VOLUNTEER, MENTOR, HOPEFUL.

"She is a *queen*," Parker whispered, unable to look away, to move, to breathe.

In that moment Parker saw more than just a portrait—
she saw a road before her with endless possibilities.

Suddenly, Parker felt a small hand in hers,
and the spell was broken.

"Come look, Ava," she said, putting
her arm around her little sister
and standing tall.

For Parker Curry was feeling powerful and strong, and even though she hadn't moved . . .

INSIDE
SHE WAS
DANCING.

ACKNOWLEDGMENTS

TO MARQUIS, MY HUSBAND, while our journey in parenting has only truly just begun, it's been quite the ride thus far, and there is nobody I would rather share this journey with. I know this next chapter in our life is going to be one we never forget. Love you.

Papi and Nana, Grand-mère, and CynD, your unconditional love, encouragement, and guidance over the years couldn't have prepared me better for both the present and the future that lies ahead. Thank you for the priceless lessons and wisdom you've shared over the years.

To my little sister, Jana Curry, I remember us excitedly discussing the unveiling of the Obama portraits at the National Portrait Gallery, a place we frequented often with Parker. That rainy day in March, the day before you would board a plane to relocate to San Francisco, we explored the halls of NPG not knowing the profound impact that that day's particular visit would have on people around the world. Thank you for always supporting and encouraging my desire to expose my children to new places, spaces, and ideas that aren't necessarily deemed child-friendly and for loving my children as your own.

Antranig Balian and Kirsten Neuhaus, how do I say thank you for taking a chance on pitching my three-year-old's inspirational story? There aren't words that could express how grateful I am to both of you for your support, knowledge, long-distance phone calls, and e-mails around the clock, and for making this experience nothing less than magical. We're lucky to have you both on our team and couldn't have hoped for better partners in sharing our story.

Mara Anastas, because of your thoughtful and insightful leadership, this book is more than I could have ever imagined it would be, and I am honored to have had the opportunity for work with the amazing team of individuals you curated to help share our story with the world.

Laura DiSiena, your loving art direction has taken this story to an inspired level I never could have imagined; Rebecca Vitkus, for your thoughtful attention to every last detail and nuance; and Julie Doebler, for making sure the book is a beautiful, enduring keepsake.

Brittany Jackson, your art has not only captured my heart, but I know it will enchant and enrich everyone who is lucky to experience it. Each and every page is magically illustrated, and you were undoubtedly the perfect person to bring our story to life. I am forever grateful!

Karen Nagel, from the moment I saw your initial e-mail about my idea for Parker's book, I knew that Simon & Schuster would become our book's home. There has always been something so poetic, precise, and magical about your understanding of what I wanted this book to convey and how I wanted it to make those reading it feel. From our late-night chats to our visit to NPG, the entire process of writing this book and bringing it to life with illustrations has been nothing less than a dream come true. Thank you for your patience, friendship, guidance, and support over the last year. You are one of the most insightful and inspiring creatives I've ever had the pleasure of knowing and working with, and my sincerest prayer is that if God sees fit, we'll have the opportunity to collaborate on more projects in the future that will inspire generations to come. דעונ להיות (*bashert*)

A NOTE FROM AMY SHERALD

Seeing Parker Curry gaze up at former First Lady Michelle Obama in the National Portrait Gallery took me back to my first visit to a museum in Columbus, Georgia, my hometown. It was there, for the very first time, that I saw a person in a painting by Bo Bartlett that looked like me. Up until that point, I had only seen paintings in encyclopedias. I knew I wanted to be an artist, but that painting made me realize I could actually become one.

Culture determines who counts in society and reflects the society itself. What Parker observed while looking at the portrait of the First Lady was *her own* greatness.

Without representation of all, there will be stories that are missing. When I studied art history, I observed the absence of images that reflected us as our whole selves. I see it as my responsibility to make sure that little girls and boys can walk into an institution like the Smithsonian and see that there are people who walked before them, who not only looked like them, but whose accomplishments were so great that their legacy has been archived for all to see.

Amy Sherald is an acclaimed artist best known for her official portrait of the former First Lady Michelle Obama. She received a BA in painting from Clark Atlanta University and an MFA in painting from Maryland Institute College of Art. Sherald was the first woman to win the Outwin Boochever Portrait Competition grand prize for the National Portrait Gallery in Washington, DC.

THIS BOOK CONTAINS VARIOUS PAINTINGS,
reimagined as Parker Curry experienced them during her
unforgettable and memorable visit to the National Portrait Gallery
and Smithsonian American Art Museum.

They saw prancing horses: *August Belmont and Isabel Perry*/Wouterus Verschuur. National Portrait Gallery, Smithsonian Institution; gift of Paul Mellon

Blooming flowers: *George Washington Carver*/Betsy Graves Reyneau. National Portrait Gallery, Smithsonian Institution; transfer from the Smithsonian American Art Museum; gift of the George Washington Carver Memorial Committee to the Smithsonian Institution/© Peter Edward Fayard

A bushy mustache: *Albert Einstein*/Max Westfield. National Portrait Gallery, Smithsonian Institution; gift of the artist/© Estate of Max Westfield

A shiny jeweled necklace: *Frida Kahlo*/Magda Pach. National Portrait Gallery, Smithsonian Institution

Two peacocks with red eyes: *Peacocks and Peonies*/John La Farge. Smithsonian American Art Museum, Gift of Henry A. La Farge

A basket of slimy fish: *The Chinese Fishmonger*/Theodore Wores. Smithsonian American Art Museum, Gift of Dr. Ben and A. Jess Shenson

Lots and lots of brilliant feathers: *Young Omahaw, War Eagle, Little Missouri, and Pawnees*/Charles Bird King. Smithsonian American Art Museum, Gift of Miss Helen Barlow

Frilly white tutus: *The White Ballet*/Everett Shinn. Smithsonian American Art Museum, Purchase made possible by the American Art Forum and the Luisita L. and Franz H. Denghausen Endowment

Michelle Obama: *First Lady Michelle Obama*/Amy Sherald. National Portrait Gallery, Smithsonian Institution; gift of Kate Capshaw and Steven Spielberg; Judith Kern and Kent Whealy; Tommie L. Pegues and Donald A. Capoccia; Clarence, DeLoise, and Brenda Gaines; Jonathan and Nancy Lee Kemper; The Stoneridge Fund of Amy and Marc Meadows; Robert E. Meyerhoff and Rheda Becker; Catherine and Michael Podell; Mark and Cindy Aron; Lyndon J. Barrois and Janine Sherman Barrois; The Honorable John and Louise Bryson; Paul and Rose Carter; Bob and Jane Clark; Lisa R. Davis; Shirley Ross Davis and Family; Alan and Lois Fern; Conrad and Constance Hipkins; Sharon and John Hoffman; Audrey M. Irmas; John Legend and Chrissy Teigen; Eileen Harris Norton; Helen Hilton Raiser; Philip and Elizabeth Ryan; Roselyne Chroman Swig; Josef Vascovitz and Lisa Goodman; Eileen Baird; Dennis and Joyce Black Family Charitable Foundation; Shelley Brazier; Aryn Drake-Lee; Andy and Teri Goodman; Randi Charno Levine and Jeffrey E. Levine; Fred M. Levin and Nancy Livingston, The Shenson Foundation; Monique Meloche Gallery, Chicago; Arthur Lewis and Hau Nguyen; Sara and John Schram; Alyssa Taubman and Robert Rothman

WITH GREAT THANKS AND APPRECIATION
to the National Portrait Gallery, the Smithsonian American Art Museum,
Erin Beasley, Riche Sorensen, and the estates of artists Betsy Graves Reyneau
and Max Westfield for their invaluable support of this project.